Peppa Pig

and the

Silly Sniffles

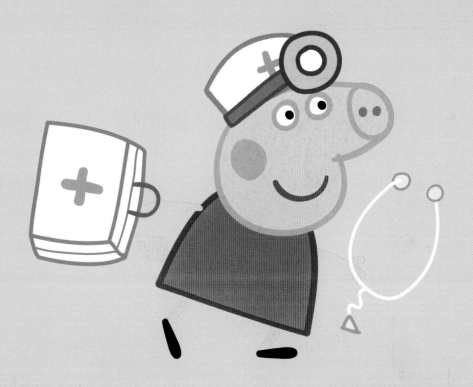

This book is based on the TV series *Peppa Pig*.
Peppa Pig is created by Neville Astley and Mark Baker.

First edition 2018

Library of Congress Catalog Card Number pending
ISBN 978-1-5362-0343-1

18 19 20 21 22 23 APS 10 9 8 7 6 5 4 3 2 1

Printed in Humen, Dongguan, China

This book was typeset in Peppa.
The illustrations were created digitally.

Candlewick Entertainment
an imprint of Candlewick Press
99 Dover Street
Somerville, Massachusetts 02144

visit us at www.candlewick.com

Peppa Pig and the
Silly Sniffles

Sniff,
sniff.

CANDLEWICK
ENTERTAINMENT

Peppa Pig and Suzy Sheep are playing store.
Suzy Sheep stocks the shelves. Peppa takes the money.

"This is a fun job," says Peppa.

Danny Dog is their first customer.

"Hello! Could I have some **cookies**, please?"

"We don't have any cookies," says Suzy,

"but we have a **toy telephone**!"

Candy Cat is next. "May I have a loaf of bread, please?"

"We don't have any bread," says Suzy. "But here's a . . .

toy house."

More and more customers come in.

Rebecca Rabbit buys a carrot.

Zoe Zebra asks for apples,
and Suzy and Peppa sell her a toy truck.

"Being a shopkeeper is
hard work!"
says Peppa.

Pedro Pony comes in next.

Achoo!

Sniff, sniff.

Cough, cough.

Pedro has the sniffles.

Poor Pedro! Peppa and Suzy don't have
anything in their shop for him.
"Suzy," says Peppa,
"let's play a new game.
We can help Pedro feel better."

Peppa and Suzy go to the dress-up boxes
and change into their new outfits.

Then Dr. Peppa and Nurse Suzy
go to work.

"Let's have a look, Pedro," says Dr. Peppa.

Peppa examines the patient.

"Oh, this is serious,"

she says.

"What should we do?"

asks Nurse Suzy.

Peppa has an idea.
She knows just what to do
to make Pedro better.

"How's that, Pedro?" asks Suzy.

Cough, cough.

"Don't worry, Pedro," says Peppa.
"I have another idea!"

"Are you feeling better yet, Pedro?"
asks Suzy.

Achoo!

Achoo!

Cough!

"Not yet."

Achoo!

"OK, I have an extra-special treatment," says Peppa.

"Great idea, Peppa!" says Suzy.

"You are a very

good doctor."

ACHOO! Sniff, sniff, sniff.

Cough, cough.

Peppa and Suzy try again.

They are giving Pedro a cast!
"But Peppa," says Pedro,
"I don't have a broken leg. I have . . .

the sniffles!" Achoo!

Sniff, sniff.

But everyone wants to see and sign Pedro's cast.

Candy Cat draws a flower.

Danny Dog draws a parrot.

Zoe Zebra draws Mr. Potato.

Dr. Peppa draws a muddy puddle.

"Oh, I think I have the sniffles, too," says Candy Cat.

"Can you help me, Dr. Peppa?"

"Yes, me too," says Danny Dog.

"I need a cast!"

Everyone wants
Dr. Peppa to help!

"I still have the sniffles," says Pedro.
"But I feel much better!"
Thank you, Nurse Suzy!
Thank you, Dr. Peppa!